READING CHAMPION

Show and Tell

by Damian Harvey and Louise Forshaw

W

Bindi was getting ready
for school.

"Miss Tam said I have to take
something for Show and Tell
today," she said.

"What will you take?" said Dad.

"I don't know," said Bindi.

"Can you help me?"

Dad went to look for something
for Bindi to take to school.
He came back with
a long brown box.

"You can take this," he said,
and he gave the box to Bindi.
"What's inside?" said Bindi.
"You will have to wait and see,"
said Dad.

On the way to school, Dad and Bindi saw Tess.

"What have you got in your box?" said Tess.

"I don't know," said Bindi.

"Dad said that I have to

wait and see."

"Is it your pet rat?" said Tess.

"Miss Tam will not be happy

if it is," said Bindi.

"She will not want a rat in school."

At school, Bindi saw
Milly and Billy.
"What have you got
in your box?" said Milly.
"Dad said that I have to
wait and see," said Bindi.

"I think it's a car," said Milly.

"I think it's a toy robot with bright red eyes," said Billy.

Bindi put her box
on Miss Tam's table.
"What have you got
in your box?" said Miss Tam.

"I think it's a rabbit," said Jamil.

"I think it's a bear," said Sol.

"Let's have a look," said Miss Tam.

Bindi opened the box.

Everyone looked inside.

"The box is empty!"

they all cried.

Bindi looked into the box.

"No, it isn't!" she said.

"Look! There's a **hole** in it!"

And everyone laughed.

Story trail

Start at the beginning of the story trail. Ask your child to retell the story in their own words, pointing to each picture in turn to recall the sequence of events.

Start

Independent Reading

This series is designed to provide an opportunity for your child to read on their own. These notes are written for you to help your child choose a book and to read it independently.

In school, your child's teacher will often be using reading books which have been banded to support the process of learning to read. Use the book band colour your child is reading in school to help you make a good choice. *Show and Tell* is a good choice for children reading at Green Band in their classroom to read independently.

The aim of independent reading is to read this book with ease, so that your child enjoys the story and relates it to their own experiences.

About the book

Bindi has to take something in for Show and Tell. Dad gets her a box to take in, and everyone tries to guess what might be inside it.

Before reading

Help your child to learn how to make good choices by asking: "Why did you choose this book? Why do you think you will enjoy it?" Look at the cover together and ask: "What do you think the story will be about?" Support your child to think of what they already know about the story context. Read the title aloud and ask: "What do you think might be in the box on the cover?"

Remind your child that they can try to sound out the letters to make a word if they get stuck.

Decide together whether your child will read the story independently or read it aloud to you.

During reading

If reading aloud, support your child if they hesitate or ask for help by telling the word. Remind your child of what they know and what they can do independently.

If reading to themselves, remind your child that they can come and ask for your help if stuck.

After reading

Support comprehension by asking your child to tell you about the story. Use the story trail to encourage your child to retell the story in the right sequence, in their own words.

Help your child think about the messages in the book that go beyond the story and ask: "Why do you think Dad gave Bindi a box with a hole in it?"

Give your child a chance to respond to the story: "Did you have a favourite part? Do you have Show and Tell at your school? If so, have you taken anything in from home to talk about?"

Extending learning

Help your child understand the story structure by using the same story context and adding different elements. "Let's make up a new story about something else unexpected that Bindi has taken in for Show and Tell. What will Bindi take into school? What might her friends guess she has taken in this time?"

In the classroom, your child's teacher may be teaching polysyllabic words (words with more than one syllable). There are many in this book that you could look at with your child, for example: some/thing, to/day, happ/y, ro/bot, rabb/it, ta/ble, in/side, no/thing, eve/ry/one.

Franklin Watts
First published in Great Britain in 2020
by The Watts Publishing Group

Series Editors: Jackie Hamley and Melanie Palmer
Series Advisors: Dr Sue Bodman and Glen Franklin
Series Designer: Peter Scoulding

A CIP catalogue record for this book is
available from the British Library.

ISBN 978 1 4451 7080 0 (hbk)
ISBN 978 1 4451 7079 4 (pbk)
ISBN 978 1 4451 7081 7 (library ebook)

Printed in China

Franklin Watts
An imprint of
Hachette Children's Group
Part of The Watts Publishing Group
Carmelite House
50 Victoria Embankment
London EC4Y 0DZ

An Hachette UK Company
www.hachette.co.uk

www.franklinwatts.co.uk

FSC
www.fsc.org
MIX
Paper from
responsible sources
FSC® C104740